3-26-22

CREATIVE ARTWORK

NOTED.

TW/DG

The Shape of My Heart

Mark Sperring

illustrated by Alys Paterson

BLOOMSBURY

NEW YORK LONDON NEW DELHI SYDNEY

This is the shape that we are.

The shape of you
and me.

This is the shape of our eyes.

And these are the shapes we might see.

clink!

tick-tock!

raaaa!

crunch!

wibble-wobble!

yummy!

splish-splash!

This is the shape of the sun,
coming up to brighten our day.

And these are the shapes that chirp and tweet…

tweet!

flitter!

tweet!

flutter!

tweet!

and flitter-flutter away.

HELLO!

This is the shape of our mouths.

hello!

Hi!

hello!

HELLO!

hello!

hi!

Now, what would
you like to eat?

Something hot

or something cold?

Something savory

or sweet?

This is the shape of my shoes.

And this
is the shape
of your feet.

brrrm!

brrrm!

And these are the shapes that pass us by...

beep!

beep!

chu

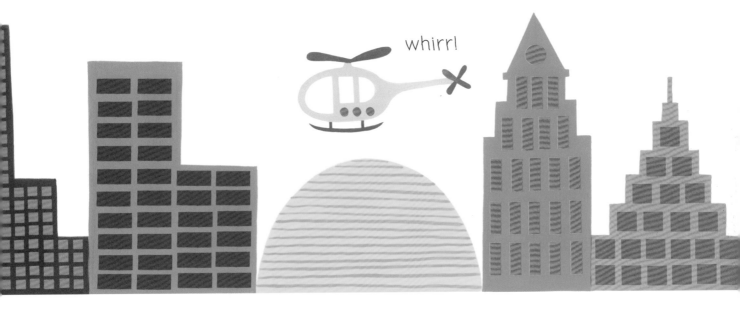

whirr!

beep!

beep!

on a noisy, busy street.

vroom!

vroom!

chug!

beep!

This is the shape of my hand,
the hand you hold on to.

Where are we going, and what will we see?

roar!

Let's look at the
shapes at the zoo!

snap!

grrrr!

hissssss!

flap!
flap!

squeak!

arr, arr!

This is the shape I
hear you with.

LET'S BE ON OUR WAY!

And this is the shape we come back to . . .

at the very end of the day.

This is the shape of the pillow where you lay your sleepy head.

And this is the shape
of the toy that you
cuddle up with in bed.

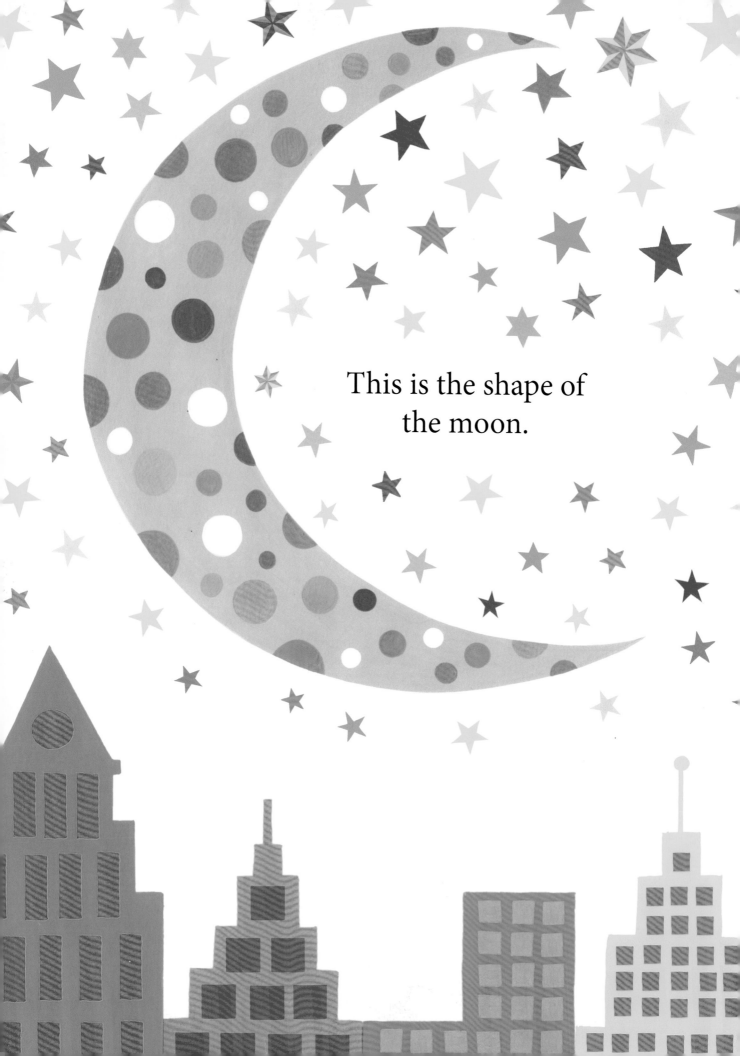

This is the shape of
the moon.

And these are the shapes
of the stars . . .

And this is the shape
I love you with.

This is the shape
of my heart.

For you . . . to read with those you love
~M. S.

For Mum, Dad, Bob, and Gran with all my love
~A. P.

Published in Great Britain in January 2013 by Bloomsbury Publishing Plc
Published in the United States of America in December 2012
by Bloomsbury Books for Young Readers
www.bloomsburykids.com

For information about permission to reproduce selections from this book, write to
Permissions, Bloomsbury BFYR, 175 Fifth Avenue, New York, New York 10010

Library of Congress Cataloging-in-Publication Data
available upon request
ISBN 978-1-59990-962-2 (hardcover) • ISBN 978-1-59990-963-9 (reinforced)

Art created with mixed media
Typeset in Minion Pro

Printed in China by C&C Offset Printing Co., Ltd., Shenzhen, Guangdong
2 4 6 8 10 9 7 5 3 1 (hardcover)
2 4 6 8 10 9 7 5 3 1 (reinforced)

All papers used by Bloomsbury Publishing, Inc., are natural, recyclable products
made from wood grown in well-managed forests. The manufacturing processes
conform to the environmental regulations of the country of origin.

Where Are My Onions?

First published simultaneously in
Great Britain and Canada in 1997 by
Tradewind Books Limited
29 Lancaster Park, Richmond, Surrey TW10 6AB England,
& Tradewind Books Limited
2216 Stephens Street, Vancouver, British Columbia V6K 3W6 Canada.

Design by Rose Cowles (Canada)
and Glynn Pickerill (London)

Originated in Hong Kong by Bright Arts HK Limited

Printed in Singapore

10 9 8 7 6 5 4 3 2 1

Cataloguing-in-Publication Data for this book is
available from the British Library

Canadian Cataloguing in Publication Data

Sarmonpal, Paulette, 1959-
Where are my onions?

ISBN 1-896580-08-4

I. Vignale, Silvia, 1958. II. Title
PZ7.S87Wh 1997   j823'.914   C96-910151-1

Where Are My Onions?

by **Paulette Sarmonpal**

Illustrated by **Silvia Vignale**

London/Vancouver

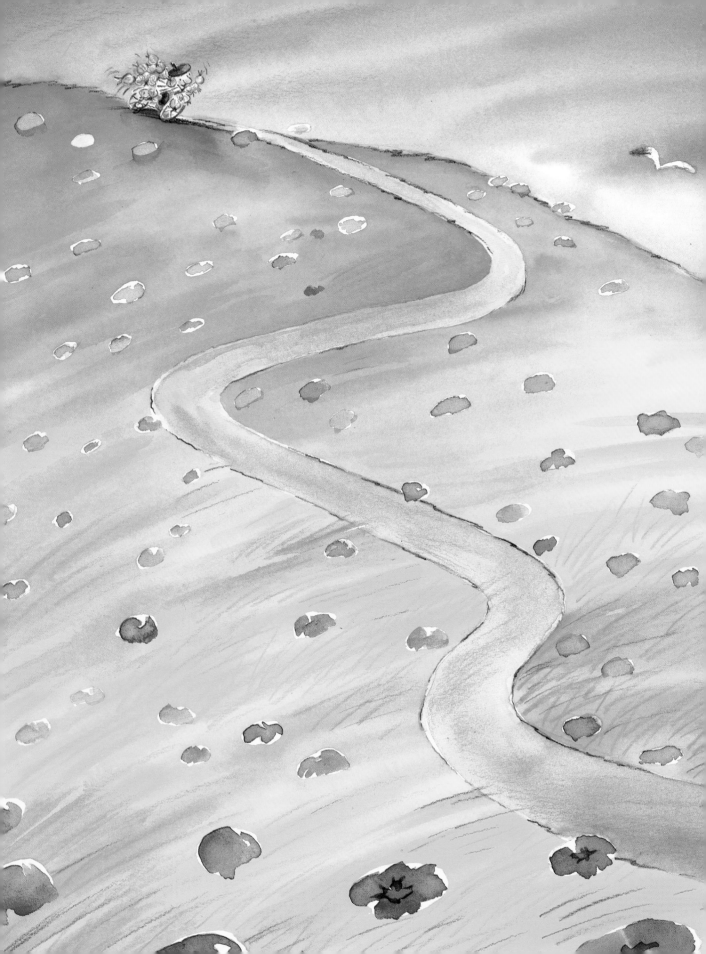

Jean-Claude was the onion man.
He rode all the way from Dieppe on
his very old-fashioned black bicycle
with its large silver bell.

Of course, he didn't ride across the channel.

Oh, no! He caught the ferry and then
rode the rest of the way to London.

You never knew when Jean-Claude
would arrive, but he certainly
knew when people were running
out of onions. How he knew I
cannot tell, but he said his nose
could sniff out all the places
with no onions left.
You see, Jean-Claude had a very
large and fine nose.
He could even tell you where an
onion had been grown from
anywhere in the world
with just one

sniff.

Even one which came from
as far away as China.

As he rode his creaky old bicycle
up the hill, he would call out
in his cheery voice,

"*Oignons,*
Oignons."

(That's French for onions.)

There were strings of onions around his
neck, strings of onions over his cross-bar
and strings of onions hanging from his arms.
And peeping out from all of those onions,
you could barely see the top of his head with
his black felt beret perched on top. But one
thing you could *always* see was his nose.

When Jamie's mother heard the onion man, she rushed to the open window and called out " *Monsieur, Monsieur, je voudrais trois cordes, s'il vous plaît!* "

Jamie always laughed when his mother tried to speak French, but Jean-Claude was always very polite and knew exactly what she meant.

Jamie loved to carry the long strings of onions home and hang them on a hook in the kitchen.

Jamie's cat, Quizz, loved to run out and sniff the onions and wrap his tail around the onion man's leg. Unfortunately the onion man did **not** like cats playing with his onions.

Quizz was a peculiar cat who never
gave up trying to chase the onions.
He thought they were the most
interesting things he had ever seen.
Some onion skins were shiny and
smooth, some were crispy and
flaking off and some made nice
crackling, scrunching noises.
Onions were such good round shapes
for rolling along the ground.
With so many on a string, they pull
and tangle up in your paws.

Quizz loved everything about onions and was always trying to get a string for himself.

One windy autumn day when the leaves were tumbling down from the trees, the onion man appeared. He rang his bell and all the children ran out to meet him.

"Oignons!"

"Oignons, oignons!"

the children shouted
in a nice French accent.

Jean-Claude loved children.
It was only cats he was wary of
because of one particular cat who
was always chasing his onions.

Suddenly, it began to rain and stray
newspapers whipped along the ground,
whirled up and landed smack in
Jean Claude's face. The papers were so
wet, and the wind was blowing so
fiercely, that they stuck to his nose.
He could barely breathe, let alone
peel them off his face.

Finally, Jean-Claude freed himself from the tangles of newspapers, picked up his bicycle and discovered that

all his onions ...

had disappeared!

Every single string.

Every single onion.

He sat down on a wall and cried out ...

"Où sont mes oignons?"

(French for, "Where are my onions?")

Well, the rain had stopped and everyone peeped out their windows to see that Jean-Claude was very upset.

Mothers, children, the postman and even a builder came out to help him search.

They looked behind trees, on branches,

in bins

and backyards.

They even looked
in the park and under
piles of leaves.

The big search came to an end and not

one

single

solitary

onion

was found.

So everyone threw their arms up in the
air and declared it to be a great mystery.

"Why don't you come in for a cup of tea and warm up a bit, Jean-Claude?" Jamie's mother said, trying to cheer him up.
"*Mais oui, Madame!*" Jean-Claude said, taking in a deep breath and letting out a long sigh.
"*Merci bien, Madame. Merci bien.*"
When Jean-Claude took in another deep breath with his very large, fine nose, he smelled something quite familiar.

" *Mes oignons,*"

he cried.

And away he went, nose in the air, with everyone following behind.

Jean-Claude had no idea where he was going.
But he *did* know that, without a doubt, his nose
would not fail him. So he
continued to follow his nose
up Jamie's front steps,
through the front door, up
another flight of stairs,
down a long corridor and
into Jamie's bedroom,
where to everyone's
surprise ...

Quizz lay sleeping on the biggest pillow of onions anyone had ever seen.

To celebrate, Jamie's mother invited
in all the neighbours who had helped
to look for Jean-Claude's missing
onions and made a big pot of onion
soup for everyone to share.
When they all remarked how simply
delicious the soup tasted,
Jean-Claude beamed with pride
and blurted out,

"Ce sont mes oignons!"

(It's my onions!)